THE ADDAMS FAMILY

WEDNESDAY'S LIBRARY

DELIGHTFULLY DARK QUOTES
AND GOTHIC TALES
FROM ONE GRIM GIRL

Written by
ALEXANDRA WEST & CALLIOPE GLASS

HARPER
An Imprint of HarperCollinsPublishers

MGM

UA   MGM

www.harpercollinschildrens.com

Library of Congress Control Number: 2019941461

ISBN 978-0-06-294684-3

Designed by Joe Merkel

19 20 21 22 23   LSCC   10 9 8 7 6 5 4 3 2 1

❖

First Edition

CONTENTS

WEDNESDAY'S
READING LIST

FRANKENSTEIN; OR, THE MODERN PROMETHEUS
by Mary Wollstonecraft Shelley

HEART OF DARKNESS
by Joseph Conrad

THE STRANGE CASE OF
DR. JEKYLL AND MR. HYDE
by Robert Louis Stevenson

THE TRAGEDY OF MACBETH
by William Shakespeare

THE DIVINE COMEDY
by Dante Alighieri

"THE LEGEND OF SLEEPY HOLLOW"
by Washington Irving

JANE EYRE
by Charlotte Brontë

LES MISÉRABLES
by Victor Hugo

POEMS
by Emily Dickinson

THE CASTLE OF OTRANTO
by Horace Walpole

HAMLET, PRINCE OF DENMARK
by William Shakespeare

PARADISE LOST
by John Milton

THE WORKS OF EDGAR ALLAN POE
by Edgar Allan Poe

WEDNESDAY'S
LIBRARY

LITERATURE

THERE'S NOTHING I LOVE MORE IN THIS
WORLD THAN TORMENT. AND NO ONE
UNDERSTANDS THAT MORE THAN MY
FAVORITE AUTHOR, EDGAR ALLAN POE.
HIS POEM "THE RAVEN" IS WHAT
I BASED MY MOST RECENT SCHOOL
PROJECT ON. I DON'T THINK MY
TEACHER ENJOYED IT MUCH.

SHE SEEMS TO DETERIORATE BY
THE DAY. LOOKS LIKE MY
RAVEN IS DOING HIS JOB.

THE RAVEN

Once upon a midnight dreary, while I pondered, weak and weary,
Over many a quaint and curious volume of forgotten lore—
While I nodded, nearly napping, suddenly there came a tapping,
As of some one gently rapping, rapping at my chamber door.
"'Tis some visitor," I muttered, "tapping at my chamber door—
Only this and nothing more."

Ah, distinctly I remember it was in the bleak December;
And each separate dying ember wrought its ghost upon the floor.
Eagerly I wished the morrow;—vainly I had sought to borrow
From my books surcease of sorrow—sorrow for the lost Lenore—
For the rare and radiant maiden whom the angels name Lenore—
Nameless *here* for evermore.

And the silken, sad, uncertain rustling of each purple curtain
Thrilled me—filled me with fantastic terrors never felt before;
So that now, to still the beating of my heart, I stood repeating
"'Tis some visitor entreating entrance at my chamber door—
Some late visitor entreating entrance at my chamber door;—
    This it is and nothing more."

Presently my soul grew stronger; hesitating then no longer,

"Sir," said I, "or Madam, truly your forgiveness I implore;

But the fact is I was napping, and so gently you came rapping,

And so faintly you came tapping, tapping at my chamber door,

That I scarce was sure I heard you"—here I opened wide the door;—

      Darkness there and nothing more.

Deep into that darkness peering, long I stood there wondering, fearing,

Doubting, dreaming dreams no mortal ever dared to dream before;

But the silence was unbroken, and the stillness gave no token,

And the only word there spoken was the whispered word, "Lenore?"

This I whispered, and an echo murmured back the word, "Lenore!"—

      Merely this and nothing more.

Back into the chamber turning, all my soul within me burning,
Soon again I heard a tapping somewhat louder than before.
"Surely," said I, "surely that is something at my window lattice;
Let me see, then, what thereat is, and this mystery explore—
Let my heart be still a moment and this mystery explore;—
     'Tis the wind and nothing more!"

Open here I flung the shutter, when, with many a flirt and flutter,
In there stepped a stately Raven of the saintly days of yore;
Not the least obeisance made he; not a minute stopped or stayed he;
But, with mien of lord or lady, perched above my chamber door—
Perched upon a bust of Pallas just above my chamber door—
     Perched, and sat, and nothing more.

Then this ebony bird beguiling my sad fancy into smiling,

By the grave and stern decorum of the countenance it wore,

"Though thy crest be shorn and shaven, thou," I said, "art sure no craven,

Ghastly grim and ancient Raven wandering from the Nightly shore—

Tell me what thy lordly name is on the Night's Plutonian shore!"

      Quoth the Raven "Nevermore."

Much I marvelled this ungainly fowl to hear discourse so plainly,

Though its answer little meaning—little relevancy bore;

For we cannot help agreeing that no living human being

Ever yet was blessed with seeing bird above his chamber door—

Bird or beast upon the sculptured bust above his chamber door,

      With such name as "Nevermore."

But the Raven, sitting lonely on the placid bust, spoke only

That one word, as if his soul in that one word he did outpour.

Nothing farther then he uttered—not a feather then he fluttered—

Till I scarcely more than muttered "Other friends have flown before—

On the morrow *he* will leave me, as my Hopes have flown before."

      Then the bird said "Nevermore."

Startled at the stillness broken by reply so aptly spoken,

"Doubtless," said I, "what it utters is its only stock and store

Caught from some unhappy master whom unmerciful Disaster

Followed fast and followed faster till his songs one burden bore—

Till the dirges of his Hope that melancholy burden bore

      Of 'Never—nevermore'."

But the Raven still beguiling all my fancy into smiling,

Straight I wheeled a cushioned seat in front of bird, and bust and door;

Then, upon the velvet sinking, I betook myself to linking

Fancy unto fancy, thinking what this ominous bird of yore—

What this grim, ungainly, ghastly, gaunt, and ominous bird of yore

      Meant in croaking "Nevermore."

This I sat engaged in guessing, but no syllable expressing

To the fowl whose fiery eyes now burned into my bosom's core;

This and more I sat divining, with my head at ease reclining

On the cushion's velvet lining that the lamp-light gloated o'er,

But whose velvet-violet lining with the lamp-light gloating o'er,

      She shall press, ah, nevermore!

Then, methought, the air grew denser, perfumed from an unseen censer
Swung by Seraphim whose foot-falls tinkled on the tufted floor.
"Wretch," I cried, "thy God hath lent thee—by these angels he hath sent thee
Respite—respite and nepenthe from thy memories of Lenore;
Quaff, oh quaff this kind nepenthe and forget this lost Lenore!"

      Quoth the Raven "Nevermore."

"Prophet!" said I, "thing of evil!—prophet still, if bird or devil!—
Whether Tempter sent, or whether tempest tossed thee here ashore,
Desolate yet all undaunted, on this desert land enchanted—
On this home by Horror haunted—tell me truly, I implore—
Is there—*is* there balm in Gilead?—tell me—tell me, I implore!"

      Quoth the Raven "Nevermore."

"Prophet!" said I, "thing of evil!—prophet still, if bird or devil!

By that Heaven that bends above us—by that God we both adore—

Tell this soul with sorrow laden if, within the distant Aidenn,

It shall clasp a sainted maiden whom the angels name Lenore—

Clasp a rare and radiant maiden whom the angels name Lenore."

      Quoth the Raven "Nevermore."

"Be that word our sign of parting, bird or fiend!" I shrieked, upstarting—

"Get thee back into the tempest and the Night's Plutonian shore!

Leave no black plume as a token of that lie thy soul hath spoken!

Leave my loneliness unbroken!—quit the bust above my door!

Take thy beak from out my heart, and take thy form from off my door!"

      Quoth the Raven "Nevermore."

And the Raven, never flitting, still is sitting, *still* is sitting

On the pallid bust of Pallas just above my chamber door;

And his eyes have all the seeming of a demon's that is dreaming,

And the lamp-light o'er him streaming throws his shadow on the floor;

And my soul from out that shadow that lies floating on the floor

    Shall be lifted—nevermore!

—Edgar Allan Poe
"THE RAVEN,"
THE WORKS OF EDGAR ALLAN POE

THE RAVEN
REMINDS ME OF
THE GAMES I PLAY
WITH PUGSLEY.

*"Behind every exquisite
thing that existed,
there was something tragic."*

—*Oscar Wilde*
THE PICTURE OF DORIAN GRAY

THAT'S WHY I LOVE ART.
THE SCENES OF WAR AND VIOLENCE MAKE
PERFECT HOME DÉCOR.

"Beware;
for I am fearless,
and therefore
powerful."

—*Mary Wollstonecraft Shelley*
FRANKENSTEIN; OR,
THE MODERN PROMETHEUS

THIS IS A GREAT REMINDER THAT FEAR
IS A VERY IMPORTANT EMOTION
WHEN IT COMES TO ONE'S
PERSONAL SAFETY.

"I am thy father's spirit;
Doom'd for a certain term
to walk the night,
And, for the day,
confin'd to waste in fires
Till the foul crimes done
in my days of nature
Art burnt and
purg'd away."

—*William Shakespeare*
HAMLET

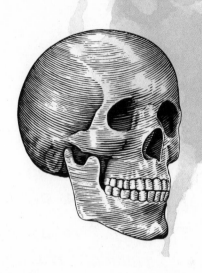

HAMLET IS ONE OF MY FAVORITE PLAYS.

IT'S SO GLOOMY.
IT HAS SO MANY GHOSTS.

*"Today I'll bake; tomorrow I'll brew.
Then I'll fetch the queen's new child.
It is good that no one knows
Rumpelstiltskin is my name."*

—Jacob Grimm and Wilhelm Grimm
"RUMPELSTILTSKIN,"
THE GRIMM BROTHERS'
CHILDREN'S AND HOUSEHOLD TALES

HOW TERRIBLY
EXCITING ARE THESE
WORDS FROM THE
CROOKED OLD
RUMPELSTILTSKIN?

THEY NEVER FAIL TO SEND SHIVERS
DOWN MY SPINE WHENEVER I READ THEM.

"The one candle was dying out: the room was full of moonlight. My heart beat fast and thick: I heard its throb. Suddenly it stood still to an inexpressible feeling that thrilled it through, and passed at once to my head and extremities. The feeling was not like an electric shock, but it was quite as sharp, as strange, as startling: it acted on my senses as if their utmost activity hitherto had been but torpor, from which they were now summoned and forced to wake. They rose expectant: eye and ear waited while the flesh quivered on my bones."

—*Charlotte Brontë*
JANE EYRE

FEAR IS SUCH A POWERFUL EMOTION, ISN'T IT? IT EVEN HAS THE ABILITY TO CHANGE ONE'S PHYSICAL APPEARANCE.

I MEAN, LOOK AT UNCLE FESTER.

"*Life,*
although it may only be
an accumulation of anguish,
is dear to me,
and I will defend it."

—*Mary Wollstonecraft Shelley*
FRANKENSTEIN; OR,
THE MODERN PROMETHEUS

FRANKENSTEIN'S MONSTER HAS AN OPTIMISM THAT I HAVE TROUBLE RELATING TO. BUT I AGREE WITH THE IDEA THAT LIFE IS AN ACCUMULATION OF ANGUISH.

"Upon the reading of this letter, I made sure my colleague was insane; but till that was proved beyond the possibility of doubt, I felt bound to do as he requested."

—Robert Louis Stevenson
THE STRANGE CASE OF
DR. JEKYLL AND MR. HYDE

I WOULD ALSO FOLLOW THE
DIRECTIVES OF INSANE PEOPLE.
THEY TEND TO BE THE MOST LEVELHEADED
PEOPLE IN THE ROOM.

"*We live in the flicker—
may it last as long
as the old earth keeps rolling!
But darkness
was here yesterday.*"

—*Joseph Conrad*
HEART OF DARKNESS

CONRAD IS REMINDING US THAT
THERE WOULD BE NO LIGHT WITHOUT
DARKNESS. THIS IS
EXACTLY WHAT I'VE BEEN
TRYING TO TELL
EVERYONE!
I AM THE
DARKNESS;
WITHOUT ME YOU'D
BE NOTHING.

*"Solitude sometimes
is best society."*

—*John Milton*
PARADISE LOST

HOW CAN ONE BE
LONELY WITH A
MIND LIKE MINE?

*"By the pricking of my thumbs,
Something wicked this way comes."*

—William Shakespeare
THE TRAGEDY OF MACBETH

WITCHES. BLOOD.
IMPENDING DEVASTATION.

IT'S AS IF WILLIAM
SHAKESPEARE WERE
WRITING ABOUT MY LIFE.

*"In olden times
when wishing still helped one,
there lived a king
whose daughters were all beautiful,
but the youngest was so beautiful
that the sun itself,
which has seen so much,
was astonished whenever
it shone in her face."*

—Jacob Grimm and Wilhelm Grimm
"THE FROG KING,"
THE GRIMM BROTHERS'
CHILDREN'S AND HOUSEHOLD TALES

ONLY TWO WRITERS AS GRIM AS
THE GRIMM BROTHERS COULD BEGIN
A STORY LIKE THIS. THIS STORY
ACTUALLY INSPIRED MY LATEST SCIENCE
EXPERIMENT WITH A FEW FROGS.

*"With a shriek
I bounded to the table, and grasped
the box that lay upon it ...
and from it, with a rattling sound,
there rolled out some instruments of
dental surgery, intermingled with
thirty-two small,
white and ivory-looking substances
that were scattered to and fro
about the floor."*

—Edgar Allan Poe
"BERENICE," THE WORKS OF EDGAR ALLAN POE

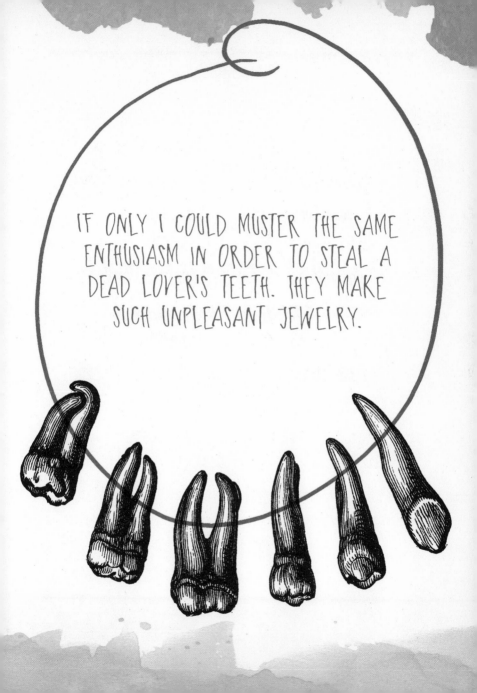

"O, full of scorpions is my mind!"

—William Shakespeare
THE TRAGEDY OF MACBETH

YOU COULD IMAGINE HOW EXCITED I GOT WHEN I FIRST READ THIS. BUT, NO, HE'S NOT TALKING ABOUT ACTUAL SCORPIONS.

"Denn die Todten reiten Schnell.
(For the dead travel fast.)"

—Bram Stoker
DRACULA

THIS WARNING ALMOST MAKES
JONATHAN HARKER TURN AROUND
AND LEAVE TRANSYLVANIA. I
PERSONALLY WOULD'VE TAKEN THIS AS
A COMPLIMENT.

"We live, as we dream—alone."

—*Joseph Conrad*
HEART OF DARKNESS

I ALWAYS FELT LIKE
JOSEPH CONRAD AND
EDGAR ALLAN POE
WOULD HAVE BEEN GOOD FRIENDS.
THEY WERE BOTH FIXATED ON
THE IDEAS OF DREAMING AND THE
MISERY OF EXISTENCE.

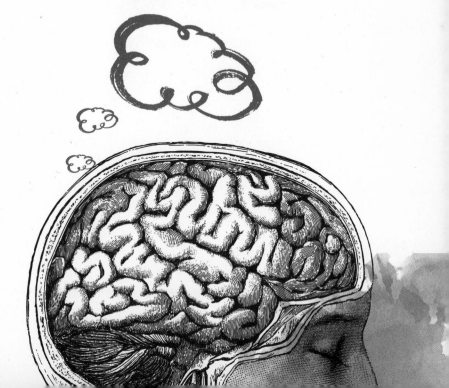

"If he be Mr. Hyde . . .
I shall be Mr. Seek."

—*Robert Louis Stevenson*
THE STRANGE CASE OF
DR. JEKYLL AND MR. HYDE

THIS IS THE ONLY PLAY ON WORDS
I'LL TOLERATE.

"She wanted—what some people want throughout life—a grief that should deeply touch her, and thus humanize and make her capable of sympathy."

—*Nathaniel Hawthorne*
THE SCARLET LETTER

NOT ONLY IS THIS BOOK A FUN ROMP INTO THE WORLD OF 17ᵀᴴ CENTURY AMERICA, BUT I FOUND IT TO ALSO BE THE PERFECT STUDY TOOL IN THE ART OF MANIPULATION.

"Once a man was sitting with his wife before their front door. They had a roasted chicken which they were about to eat together. Then the man saw that his aged father was approaching, and he hastily took the chicken and hid it, for he did not want to share it with him. The old man came, had a drink, and went away. Now the son wanted to put the roasted chicken back onto the table, but when he reached for it, it had turned into a large toad, which jumped into his face and sat there and never went away again. If anyone tried to remove it, it looked venomously at him as though it would jump into his face, so that no one dared to touch it. And the ungrateful son was forced to feed the toad every day, or else it would eat from his face. And thus he went to and fro in the world without rest."

—*Jacob Grimm and Wilhelm Grimm*
"THE UNGRATEFUL SON," THE GRIMM BROTHERS' CHILDREN'S AND HOUSEHOLD TALES

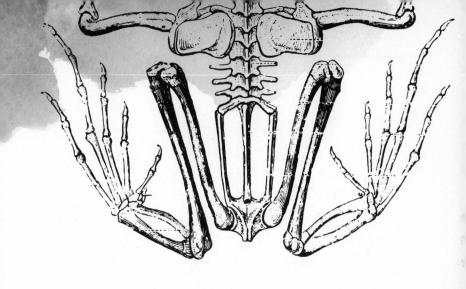

I HAVEN'T COME ACROSS A FACE—
EATING FROG IN AGES.

"If I cannot inspire love, I will cause fear..."

—*Mary Wollstonecraft Shelley*
FRANKENSTEIN; OR,
THE MODERN PROMETHEUS

THIS IS ONE OF MY FAVORITES.
HOWEVER, FOR ME, INSPIRING LOVE
NEVER CROSSED MY MIND.

"*A mind not to be chang'd
by Place or Time.*"

—John Milton
PARADISE LOST

THE MIND IS A VERY COMPELLING
THING. JUST ASK PUGSLEY; WE'VE
BEEN WORKING ON CONTROLLING
LURCH'S MIND FOR A WHILE NOW.
IT HAS PROVEN TO BE A BIT MORE
DIFFICULT THAN I ANTICIPATED.

"Listen to them—
the children of the night.
What music
they make!"

—*Bram Stoker*
DRACULA

FATHER ALWAYS QUOTES THIS LINE WHEN HE HEARS PUGSLEY AND UNCLE FESTER DIGGING UP BONES IN THE GARDEN.

*"The mind of man
is capable of
anything."*

—Joseph Conrad
HEART OF DARKNESS

IF THIS IS TRUE, THEN THE SAME MUST
BE SAID FOR WOMEN.
BUT THE MIND OF MY MOTHER IS
ALSO CAPABLE OF CONTROLLING MY
FATHER.

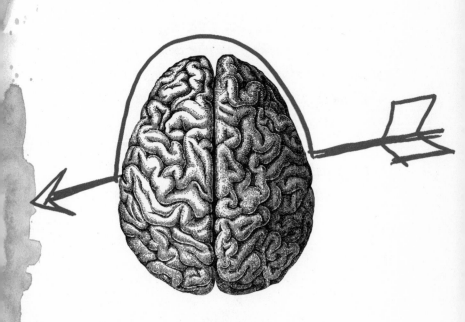

"*Returning, I had to cross before the looking-glass; my fascinated glance involuntarily explored the depth it revealed. All looked colder and darker in that visionary hollow than in reality: and the strange little figure there gazing at me, with a white face and arms specking the gloom, and glittering eyes of fear moving where all else was still, had the effect of a real spirit: I thought it like one of the tiny phantoms, half fairy, half imp, Bessie's evening stories represented as coming out of lone, ferny dells in moors, and appearing before the eyes of belated travellers.*"

—*Charlotte Brontë*
JANE EYRE

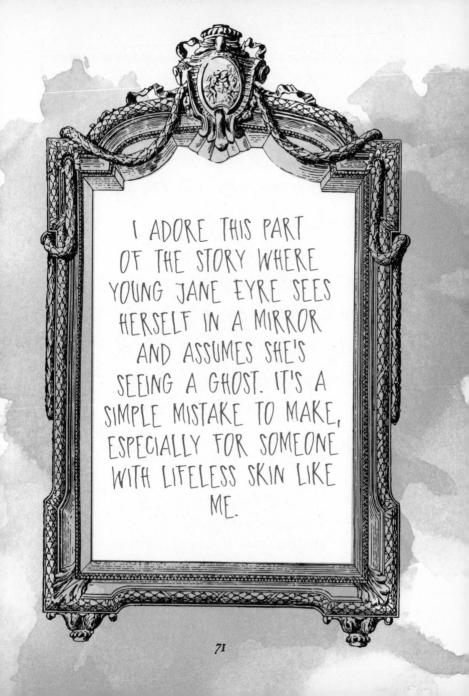

I ADORE THIS PART
OF THE STORY WHERE
YOUNG JANE EYRE SEES
HERSELF IN A MIRROR
AND ASSUMES SHE'S
SEEING A GHOST. IT'S A
SIMPLE MISTAKE TO MAKE,
ESPECIALLY FOR SOMEONE
WITH LIFELESS SKIN LIKE
ME.

*"I now observed—with what
horror . . . glittering steel, about a foot
in length from horn to horn; the horns
upward, and the under edge evidently
as keen as that of a razor. Like a
razor also, it seemed massy and heavy,
tapering from the edge into a solid
and broad structure above. It was
appended to a weighty rod of brass,
and the whole hissed
as it swung through the air."*

—Edgar Allan Poe
"THE PIT AND THE PENDULUM,"
THE WORKS OF EDGAR ALLAN POE

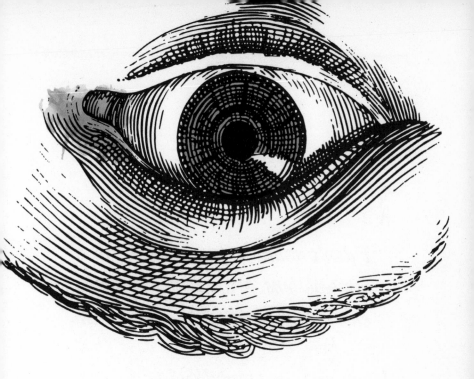

WHO DOESN'T WANT TO WAKE
UP UNDER A MASSIVE SWINGING
BLADE? PUGSLEY AND I PLAY THIS
GAME ALL THE TIME, AND HE
DOESN'T COMPLAIN HALF AS MUCH
AS THIS GUY DOES.

"*I don't want to be at the mercy of my emotions. I want to use them, to enjoy them, and to dominate them.*"

—*Oscar Wilde*
THE PICTURE OF DORIAN GRAY

I, TOO, LIKE TO BE IN CONTROL OF
MY EMOTIONS. ONE TIME . . .
I ALMOST SMIRKED.

"There, on the pendent boughs her coronet weeds
Clamb'ring to hang, an envious sliver broke;
When down her weedy trophies and herself
Fell in the weeping brook. Her clothes spread wide;
And, mermaid-like, awhile they bore her up:
Which time she chanted snatches of old tunes,
As one incapable of her own distress
Or like a creature native and endued
Unto that element: but long it could not be
Till that her garments, heavy with their drink,
Pull'd the poor wretch from her melodious lay
To muddy death."

—*William Shakespeare*
THE TRAGEDY OF HAMLET

IF YOUR DEATH IS IMMINENT, YOU MAY
AS WELL DIE LIKE OPHELIA: SINGING
LIKE A DERANGED MERMAID.

*"No man,
for any considerable period,
can wear one face to himself,
and another to the multitude,
without finally getting bewildered
as to which may be the true."*

—*Nathaniel Hawthorne*
THE SCARLET LETTER

I DON'T REALLY NEED TO WORRY ABOUT A PROBLEM LIKE THIS BECAUSE THE ONLY FACE I PRESENT TO MYSELF OR THE PUBLIC IS . . .

DISDAIN.

*" . . . knocking my knuckles through
the glass, and stretching an arm out
to seize the importunate branch;
instead of which, my fingers closed
on the fingers of a little, ice-cold hand!
The intense horror of nightmare
came over me:
I tried to draw back my arm,
but the hand clung to it, and a most
melancholy voice sobbed,
'Let me in—let me in!'"*

—Emily Brontë
WUTHERING HEIGHTS

THE BEST HOUSES HAVE GHOSTS LIVING IN THEM.

*"Through me you go
into a city of woe ...
Through me you go
amongst the lost people."*

—*Dante Alighieri*
THE DIVINE COMEDY

I LIKE THIS QUOTE VERY MUCH. I
HAVE WRITTEN THIS ON A SIGN ABOVE
MY BEDROOM DOOR.

*"Not foliage green,
but of a dusky colour,
Not branches smooth,
but gnarled and intertangled,
Not apple-trees were there,
but thorns with poison."*

—Dante Alighieri
THE DIVINE COMEDY

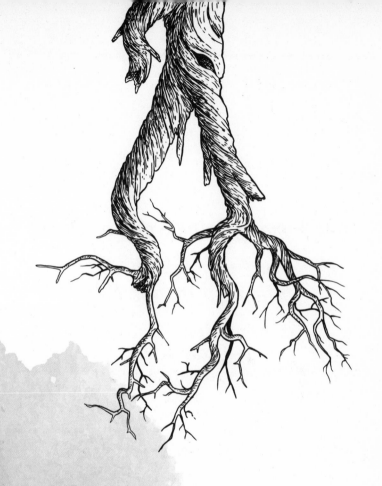

I ADORE THIS SORT OF GARDEN.

*"Men marry because they are tired;
women, because they are curious:
both are disappointed."*

—*Oscar Wilde*
THE PICTURE OF DORIAN GRAY

MY SENTIMENTS EXACTLY. WHY MARRY
WHEN YOU COULD SATIATE YOUR
CURIOSITY WITH THINGS LIKE STUDYING
POISONOUS PLANTS OR BECOMING A
COUNTRY'S FIRST FEMALE DICTATOR?

*"An air of stern, deep,
and irredeemable gloom
hung over and pervaded all."*

—*Edgar Allan Poe*
"THE FALL OF THE HOUSE OF USHER,"
THE WORKS OF EDGAR ALLAN POE

THIS IS JUST HOW A PICNIC SHOULD
BE. UNDER AIR THAT'S HEAVY
WITH GLOOM.

*"The last I saw of Count Dracula
was his kissing his hand to me;
with a red light of triumph
in his eyes."*

—Bram Stoker
DRACULA

SOMEDAY, WHEN I ACTUALLY
GET TO MEET A VAMPIRE,
I'M GOING TO HAVE SO MANY
QUESTIONS.

DOES BLOOD TASTE
GOOD? WHAT'S IT
LIKE BEING A BAT?
HOW DOES ONE GET
INTO THE BUSINESS OF . . .
IMMORTALITY?

"She had no breath for speaking.
I brought a glass full;
and as she would not drink,
I sprinkled it on her face.
In a few seconds
she stretched herself out stiff,
and turned up her eyes, while her
cheeks, at once blanched and livid,
assumed the aspect of death."

—*Emily Brontë*
WUTHERING HEIGHTS

WHAT AN EXCELLENT BEAUTY
REGIMEN. I MUST TRY THIS MYSELF.

*"Here sighs and lamentations
and loud cries
were echoing across the starless air,
so that, as soon as I set out, I wept.
Strange utterances,
horrible pronouncements,
accents of anger, words of suffering,
and voices shrill and faint,
and beating hands—"*

—Dante Alighieri
THE DIVINE COMEDY

THIS IS JUST LIKE AN ADDAMS FAMILY REUNION. OH NO. NOW I'M FEELING SENTIMENTAL.

"Dissemble no more!
I admit the deed!
Tear up the planks! Here, here!
It is the beating
of his hideous heart!"

—*Edgar Allan Poe*
"THE TELL-TALE HEART,"
THE WORKS OF EDGAR ALLAN POE

MOTHER USED TO READ THIS TO ME
AT BEDTIME! IT'S THE CLASSIC STORY
OF AN OLD MAN'S DEAD EYE TURNING
ANOTHER MAN MAD SO THAT HE
CUTS OUT THE OLD MAN'S HEART AND
THEN GOES EVEN MORE MAD WHEN
HE IS HAUNTED BY THE GHOSTLY
HEARTBEATS.

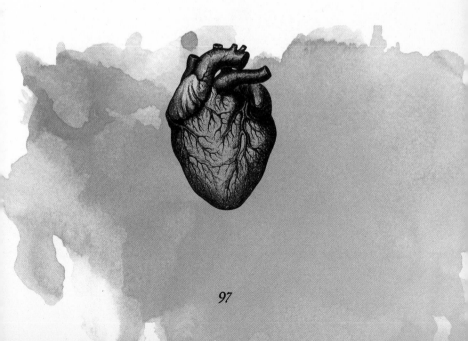

*"There comes an end to all things;
the most capacious measure
is filled at last;
and this brief condescension to evil
finally destroyed the balance
of my soul."*

—Robert Louis Stevenson
THE STRANGE CASE OF
DR. JEKYLL AND MR. HYDE

IF THERE IS ANY
GOODNESS INSIDE ME,
THEN I'M AFRAID
IT IS BROKEN.
HOW THRILLING.

"A striking similitude between the brother and sister now first arrested my attention, and Usher, divining, perhaps, my thoughts, murmured out some few words from which I learned that the deceased and himself had been twins, and that sympathies of a scarcely intelligible nature had always existed between them."

—Edgar Allan Poe

"THE FALL OF THE HOUSE OF USHER,"
THE WORKS OF EDGAR ALLAN POE

IMAGINE HOW NICE IT WOULD BE TO HAVE A BROTHER WHO WAS A GHOST. MY OWN BROTHER IS MUCH TOO ALIVE FOR MY TASTE.

*"She has man's brain—
a brain that a man should have
were he much gifted—and a
woman's heart. The good God
fashioned her for a purpose,
believe me, when He made that
so good combination."*

—*Bram Stoker*
DRACULA

I GUESS SOMEONE COULD
ALSO SAY THIS ABOUT
ME. I, TOO, HAVE A
MAN'S BRAIN AND A
WOMAN'S HEART. THEY'RE
SOMEWHERE IN THE BACK
OF MY CLOSET, I THINK.

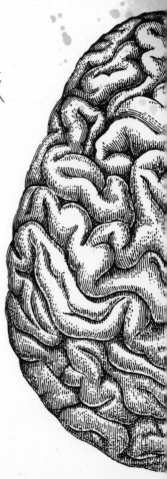

*"Look like the innocent flower,
But be the serpent under it."*

—William Shakespeare
THE TRAGEDY OF MACBETH

THIS IS ONE OF THE FIRST ADAGES
MY MOTHER EVER TAUGHT ME.
HOWEVER, I CHOOSE TO LOOK LESS
LIKE A FLOWER AND MORE LIKE
THE SERPENT.

*"Another of his sources of fearful
pleasure was to pass long winter evenings
with the old Dutch wives,
as they sat spinning by the fire, with a row
of apples roasting and spluttering along the
hearth, and listen to their
marvellous tales of ghosts and goblins,
and haunted fields, and haunted brooks, and
haunted bridges, and haunted houses, and
particularly of the headless horseman, or
Galloping Hessian of the Hollow,
as they sometimes called him."*

—*Washington Irving*
"THE LEGEND OF SLEEPY HOLLOW"

MY GRANDMOTHER WOULD DO THIS
SAME THING AND TELL US SCARY
STORIES. STRIKING FEAR IN OUR
HEARTS WAS THE ONLY THING THAT
COULD PUT US TO SLEEP AT NIGHT.

"It is true,
we shall be monsters,
cut off from all the world;
but on that account we shall be
more attached to one another."

—*Mary Wollstonecraft Shelley*
FRANKENSTEIN; OR,
THE MODERN PROMETHEUS

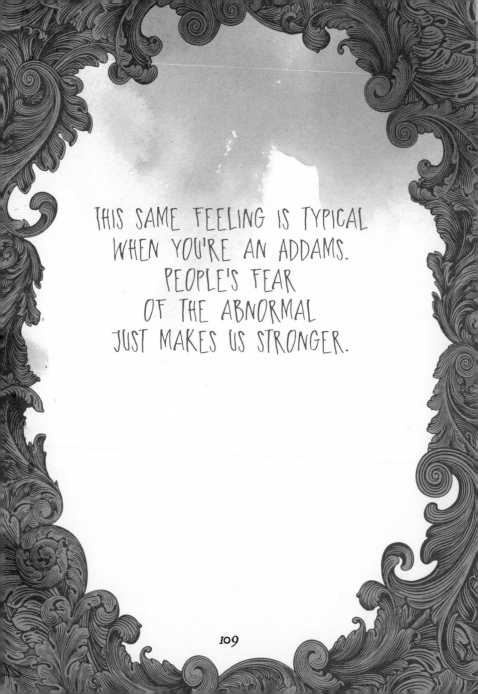

THIS SAME FEELING IS TYPICAL
WHEN YOU'RE AN ADDAMS.
PEOPLE'S FEAR
OF THE ABNORMAL
JUST MAKES US STRONGER.

*"There was an iciness,
a sinking,
a sickening of the heart."*

—Edgar Allan Poe
"THE FALL OF THE HOUSE OF USHER,"
THE WORKS OF EDGAR ALLAN POE

I ADORE THIS FEELING. THERE'S NOTHING LIKE A GOOD DREAD TO START THE DAY.

"*Stars, hide your fires!*
Let not light see my black
and deep desires."

—William Shakespeare
THE TRAGEDY OF MACBETH

I DO ALL MY BEST
WORK IN THE DARK.

"Some mention was made also of the woman in white, that haunted the dark glen at Raven Rock, and was often heard to shriek on winter nights before a storm, having perished there in the snow."

—*Washington Irving*
"THE LEGEND OF SLEEPY HOLLOW"

SHE SOUNDS LIKE THE GHOST IN
OUR WHINE CELLAR.

*"The basis of optimism
is sheer terror."*

—Oscar Wilde
THE PICTURE OF DORIAN GRAY

WHAT A ROTTEN IDEA. I KNEW THAT
THERE WERE MANY USES FOR FEAR,
BUT I NEVER THOUGHT IT COULD
ENCOURAGE . . . OPTIMISM.

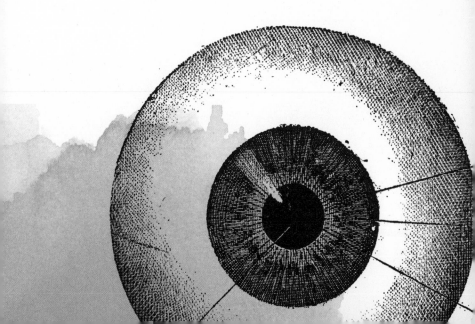

"Begone, witch, and get your things!"

—Emily Brontë
WUTHERING HEIGHTS

REMINDS ME OF SOMETHING
I READ ON A TOMBSTONE I SAW
IN ONE OF MY OLD WITCHCRAFT
HISTORY BOOKS.

"Excess of suffering,
as we have seen, had made him in
some sort a visionary."

—Victor Hugo
LES MISÉRABLES

SO SUFFERING MAKES YOU SOME SORT
OF VISIONARY? WELL, THEN, I MUST
BE SOME SORT OF PROPHET.

"He was enchained by certain superstitious impressions in regard to the dwelling which he tenanted, and whence, for many years, he had never ventured forth."

—*Edgar Allan Poe*
"THE FALL OF THE HOUSE OF USHER,"
THE WORKS OF EDGAR ALLAN POE

THIS IS VERY MUCH THE ADDAMS FAMILY WAY: FIND A CREAKY OLD HOUSE (PREFERABLY HAUNTED), MOVE IN, AND SHUT THE GATES FOREVER.

*"She had wandered, without rule or
guidance, in a moral wilderness...
Her intellect and heart had their home,
as it were, in desert places...
The scarlet letter was her passport
into regions where other women dared
not tread. Shame, Despair, Solitude!
These had been her teachers—
stern and wild ones—
and they had made her strong,
but taught her much amiss."*

—*Nathaniel Hawthorne*
THE SCARLET LETTER

SHAME, DESPAIR, SOLITUDE!
THEY ARE TEACHERS TO US ALL.

"*I heard a Fly buzz –
when I died –
The Stillness in the Room
Was like the Stillness in the Air –
Between the Heaves of Storm –*"

—*Emily Dickinson,*
"*I HEARD A FLY BUZZ – WHEN I DIED –*", POEMS

SIGH. IF ONLY I COULD WRITE A POEM ABOUT MY OWN DEATH. SOMEDAY, WHEN INSPIRATION (OR LIGHTNING) STRIKES, MAYBE I WILL.

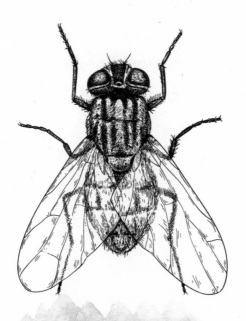

*"It is a terrible place,
the pit of darkness,
the stronghold of the blind.
It is the threshold of the abyss."*

—*Victor Hugo*
LES MISÉRABLES

I'M PRETTY SURE VICTOR HUGO ISN'T
TALKING ABOUT MY CLOSET, BUT HE
MIGHT AS WELL BE.

"In all her intercourse with society, however, there was nothing that made her feel as if she belonged to it . . . She stood apart from mortal interests, yet close beside them, like a ghost that revisits the familiar fireside, and can no longer make itself seen or felt."

—*Nathaniel Hawthorne*
THE SCARLET LETTER

SOMETIMES I FIND MYSELF FEELING
LIKE A GHOST, TOO.

BUT IN A GOOD WAY.

"I sometimes regretted that I was not handsomer: I sometimes wished to have rosy cheeks, a straight nose, and small cherry mouth; I desired to be tall, stately, and finely developed in figure; I felt it a misfortune that I was so little, so pale, and had features so irregular and so marked."

—*Charlotte Brontë*
JANE EYRE

I NEVER UNDERSTOOD WHY JANE
WOULD WANT TO LOOK SO. . .
NORMAL. HER LOOKS
ARE PERFECTLY WRETCHED.

"*I suppose that she wanted to get another proof that the place was haunted, at my expense. Well, it is— swarming with ghosts and goblins! You have reason in shutting it up, I assure you. No one will thank you for a doze in such a den!*"

—Emily Brontë
WUTHERING HEIGHTS

HOW SILLY. OBVIOUSLY, ANYONE WOULD BE HONORED TO STAY IN A HOUSE THAT'S "SWARMING WITH GHOSTS AND GOBLINS." FRANKLY, I'M JEALOUS—MY HOUSE ONLY HAS A GHOST AND A POSSESSED TREE.

"Because I could not stop for Death —
He kindly stopped for me —
The Carriage held but just Ourselves —
And Immortality."

—Emily Dickinson
"BECAUSE I COULD NOT STOP FOR DEATH —", POEMS

EMILY DICKINSON IS MY FAVORITE POET IN THE WHOLE WIDE WORLD. SHE'S MORBID, DARK, OBSESSED WITH DEATH, AND MELODRAMATIC. JUST LIKE ME.

*"We fat all creatures else to fat us,
and we fat ourselves for maggots:
your fat king and your lean beggar
is but variable service—
two dishes, but to one table."*

—*William Shakespeare*
THE TRAGEDY OF HAMLET

RICH OR POOR, NOBLE OR COMMON,
WE'RE ALL WORM FOOD IN THE END.
IT WARMS MY HEART,
IT REALLY DOES!

"I felt a Funeral, in my Brain,
And Mourners to and fro
Kept treading - treading -"

—*Emily Dickinson*
"I FELT A FUNERAL, IN MY BRAIN," POEMS

DICKINSON MAKES FUNERALS SOUND SO DRAB. FUNERALS ARE ALWAYS SUCH JOYOUS OCCASIONS FOR OUR FAMILY.

*"Your strength
is just an accident arising from
the weakness of others."*

—Joseph Conrad
HEART OF DARKNESS

PLUS, IT'S ALWAYS AN ADDED BONUS WHEN OTHERS' WEAKNESS IS THE RESULT OF YOUR OWN DEVILISH PLANS.

"*This is a bad world;
nor have I had cause to leave it
with regret.*"

—*Horace Walpole*
THE CASTLE OF OTRANTO

I BELIEVE WHAT WALPOLE IS SAYING HERE IS "LIFE IS TERRIBLE AND THEN YOU DIE."

"Safe in their Alabaster Chambers -
Untouched by Morning -
and untouched by noon -
Sleep the meek members of the Resurrection,
Rafter of Satin and Roof of Stone -"

—*Emily Dickinson*
"SAFE IN THEIR ALABASTER CHAMBERS -," POEMS

I SPENT THE NIGHT IN THE FAMILY
MAUSOLEUM ONE TIME. MOTHER SAID
I WAS VERY NAUGHTY AND MUSTN'T
DO IT AGAIN. SHE SAID IT'LL RUIN ME
FOR SLEEPING IN A REGULAR BED.

"'Climb in,' said the witch, 'and see if it is hot enough to put the bread in yet.' And when Gretel was inside, she intended to close the oven, and bake her, and eat her as well. But Gretel saw what she had in mind, so she said, 'I don't know how to do that. How can I get inside?'

"'Stupid goose,' said the old woman. 'The opening is big enough. See, I myself could get in.' And she crawled up and stuck her head into the oven. Then Gretel gave her a shove, causing her to fall in. Then she closed the iron door and secured it with a bar. The old woman began to howl frightfully. But Gretel ran away, and the godless witch burned up miserably."

—*Jacob Grimm and Wilhelm Grimm*
"HANSEL AND GRETEL,"
THE GRIMM BROTHERS'
CHILDREN'S AND HOUSEHOLD TALES

I REMEMBER WHEN I GOT TO THIS PART IN THE STORY; I WAS SO DISAPPOINTED. THE POOR WITCH . . . SHE WAS JUST HUNGRY.

"But alas! my Lord,
what is blood! what is nobility!
We are all reptiles,
miserable, sinful creatures.
It is piety alone that can distinguish us
from the dust whence we sprung,
and whither we must
return."

—Horace Walpole
THE CASTLE OF OTRANTO

HE'S ONTO SOMETHING, THIS
WALPOLE GUY. I KNOW FOR SURE
THAT PUGSLEY IS A REPTILE, AND
I'M PRETTY SURE LURCH IS FULL OF
DUST INSTEAD OF BLOOD AND GUTS
LIKE THE REST OF US.

"*The school-house, being deserted, soon fell to decay, and was reported to be haunted.*"

—*Washington Irving*
"THE LEGEND OF SLEEPY HOLLOW"

I'M HOMESCHOOLED, BUT THIS SOUNDS LIKE A GOOD ALTERNATIVE.

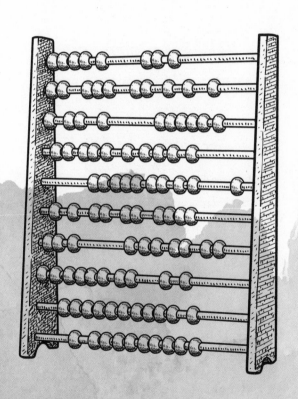

*"We were men once,
though we've become trees."*

—Dante Alighieri
THE DIVINE COMEDY

I ADORE THIS PART OF *THE DIVINE COMEDY*. I WONDER IF THIS GUY IS ONE OF THESE POOR, DOOMED SOULS CURSED TO SPEND ETERNITY TRAPPED IN HARD, UNYIELDING WOOD. SIGH.

*"She had an evil face,
smoothed by hypocrisy;
but her manners were excellent."*

—Robert Louis Stevenson
THE STRANGE CASE
OF DR. JEKYLL AND MR. HYDE

EVERY TIME
I READ THIS,
I THINK OF
MY MOTHER.

*"Excess of work exhausted
Fantine, and the small, dry cough from
which she suffered grew worse."*

—*Victor Hugo*
LES MISÉRABLES

THERE'S NOTHING BETTER THAN A SMALL, DRY COUGH THAT GETS OMINOUSLY WORSE.

*"Abashed
[he] stood,
and felt how
awful
goodness is . . ."*

—*John Milton*
PARADISE LOST

GOODNESS IS TERRIBLY AWFUL, ISN'T IT?

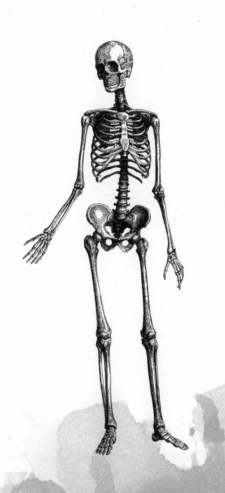

"Ichabod had been carried off by the Galloping Hessian."

—Washington Irving
"THE LEGEND OF SLEEPY HOLLOW"

WHAT DOES A GIRL HAVE TO DO TO GET A GALLOPING HESSIAN AROUND HERE?

"All is not lost—the unconquerable will,
And study of revenge, immortal hate,
And courage never to submit or yield."

—*John Milton*
PARADISE LOST

JOHN MILTON WAS THE FIRST PERSON
TO TEACH ME HOW TO
PUT TOGETHER THE PERFECT
REVENGE PLAN.

*"If they are spirits in pain,
we may ease their sufferings
by questioning them."*

—*Horace Walpole*
THE CASTLE OF OTRANTO

SEE, THIS RIGHT HERE IS *GREAT ADVICE.* DON'T RUN AWAY FROM GHOSTS . . . *TALK* TO THEM.

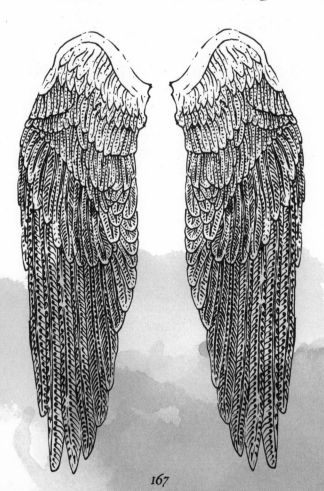

"All *that we see or seem*
Is but a dream within a dream."

Edgar Allan Poe
"A DREAM WITHIN A DREAM,"
THE WORKS OF EDGAR ALLAN POE

POE IS BASICALLY SAYING THAT LIFE
IS SO FLEETING THAT IT FEELS LIKE
A DREAM. I PERSONALLY WOULD
PREFER A NIGHTMARE,
BUT TO EACH THEIR OWN.

"My rage was without bounds; I sprang on him, impelled by all the feelings which can arm one being against the existence of another."

—*Mary Wollstonecraft Shelley*
FRANKENSTEIN; OR,
THE MODERN PROMETHEUS

<u>ALWAYS</u>
INDULGE THE RAGE.

"Fortifying herself with these reflections, and believing by what she could observe that she was near the mouth of the subterraneous cavern, she approached the door that had been opened; but a sudden gust of wind that met her at the door extinguished her lamp, and left her in total darkness."

—*Horace Walpole*
THE CASTLE OF OTRANTO

DON'T YOU HATE IT WHEN YOU'RE
RUNNING FROM A TERRIFYING
MYSTERY IN AN UNDERGROUND
TUNNEL, AND A SUDDEN WIND BLOWS
OUT YOUR LIGHT, LEAVING YOU
HELPLESS AND COMPLETELY
BLIND IN THE DARK?
NO?
ME NEITHER. I LOVE IT,
TO BE HONEST.

*"I never saw a face like it!
It was a discoloured face—it was a
savage face. I wish I could forget
the roll of the red eyes
and the fearful blackened inflation
of the lineaments!"*

—Charlotte Brontë
JANE EYRE

WHY WOULD
YOU WANT TO
FORGET A FACE
LIKE THAT?
IT SOUNDS
MAGNIFICENT
TO ME.

"They were eyes no longer, but had become those fathomless mirrors which in men who have known the depths of suffering may replace the conscious gaze, so that they no longer see reality but reflect the memory of past events."

—*Victor Hugo*
LES MISÉRABLES

SOMETIMES FATHER
GETS THAT LOOK.

IT'S QUITE
DASHING.

"*I am alone and miserable; man will not associate with me; but one as deformed and horrible as myself would not deny herself to me.*"

—*Mary Wollstonecraft Shelley*
FRANKENSTEIN; OR,
THE MODERN PROMETHEUS

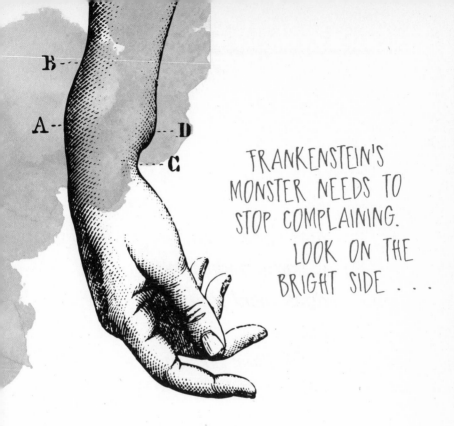

FRANKENSTEIN'S
MONSTER NEEDS TO
STOP COMPLAINING.
LOOK ON THE
BRIGHT SIDE . . .

. . . AT LEAST HE'S
ALONE AND MISERABLE.

*"That skull
had a tongue in it,
and could sing once."*

—*William Shakespeare*
HAMLET, PRINCE OF DENMARK

CLEARLY HAMLET HAS NEVER
SEEN A SKULL TALK.
I HAVE—
BUT IT GETS OLD
AFTER A WHILE.

181

ANNABEL LEE

It was many and many a year ago,
   In a kingdom by the sea,
That a maiden there lived whom you may know
   By the name of Annabel Lee;
And this maiden she lived with no other thought
   Than to love and be loved by me.

I was a child and *she* was a child,
   In this kingdom by the sea,
But we loved with a love that was more than love—
   I and my Annabel Lee—
With a love that the wingèd seraphs of Heaven
   Coveted her and me.

And this was the reason that, long ago,
  In this kingdom by the sea,
A wind blew out of a cloud, chilling
  My beautiful Annabel Lee;
So that her highborn kinsmen came
  And bore her away from me,
To shut her up in a sepulchre
  In this kingdom by the sea.

The angels, not half so happy in Heaven,
  Went envying her and me—
Yes!—that was the reason (as all men know,
  In this kingdom by the sea)
That the wind came out of the cloud by night,
  Chilling and killing my Annabel Lee.

But our love it was stronger by far than the love
　Of those who were older than we—
　Of many far wiser than we—
And neither the angels in Heaven above
　Nor the demons down under the sea
Can ever dissever my soul from the soul
　Of the beautiful Annabel Lee;

For the moon never beams, without bringing me dreams
　Of the beautiful Annabel Lee;
And the stars never rise, but I feel the bright eyes
　Of the beautiful Annabel Lee;
And so, all the night-tide, I lie down by the side
　Of my darling—my darling—my life and my bride,
　In her sepulchre there by the sea—
　In her tomb by the sounding sea.

—*Edgar Allan Poe*
"ANNABEL LEE,"
THE WORKS OF EDGAR ALLAN POE

THIS MAY BE SURPRISING, BUT I
SOMETIMES THINK THAT I WOULD LIKE
TO HAVE A ROMANCE LIKE THIS.

APPENDIX

To learn more about Wednesday's favorite books,
turn the page—at your own peril, of course.

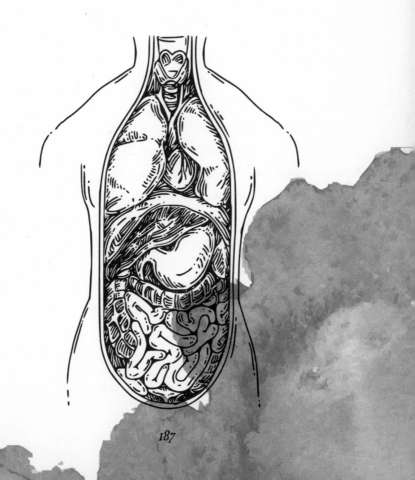

FRANKENSTEIN;
OR, THE MODERN PROMETHEUS

By Mary Wollstonecraft Shelley
Originally published anonymously in 1818

Frankenstein; or, The Modern Prometheus (so great they named it twice) is a novel inspired by the concept of galvanism, which is the idea that muscle can be reanimated using electricity. In Mary's story, a young scientist creates a creature in this way.

During "the year without a summer" in 1816, so-called because a volcano eruption filled the skies with ash, Mary traveled with friends. Her novel was actually the result of a horror story competition between her; her husband, Percy Shelley; and their friend and fellow writer Lord Byron. When Byron and Percy heard Mary's story, they encouraged her to develop it into a full-length novel, and thus *Frankenstein* was born.

It's no surprise that Wednesday enjoys reading and rereading *Frankenstein*, not just for the spooky fun, but also for new ideas for her foray into galvanism. Currently she is experimenting with frogs but plans to move on to something larger. More human.

Pages where quotations appear: 28, 36, 62, 108, 170, 178

HEART OF DARKNESS
By Joseph Conrad
Originally published in 1899

Heart of Darkness is a fascinating look into the parallels that the author, Joseph Conrad, sees between London and his experience navigating a boat up the Congo River. Conrad used his actual experience as an accidental captain of a Belgian steamer in Congo in 1890 when he wrote this novel eight years later. When the original captain of the ship became ill, Conrad stepped up and took the boat up the Lualaba River, which at the time was mainly inhabited by various African tribes.

The story of Conrad's novel follows the tale of Charles Marlow, who is telling his fellow sailors about his time in Congo, known as the "heart of Africa." Marlow paints himself as an adventurer, and his admiration for the ivory trader Kurtz quickly turns to obsession.

Wednesday may have picked up this book just for the title alone—I mean, darkness? That's her favorite color scheme. Although Wednesday would've come for the title, she stayed for the pessimistic and bleak worldview of the narrator.

Pages where quotations appear: 40, 54, 68, 142

THE STRANGE CASE OF DR. JEKYLL AND MR. HYDE

By Robert Louis Stevenson
Originally published in 1886

The Strange Case of Dr. Jekyll and Mr. Hyde is one of the most famous gothic novellas of our time, and its impact is so great, it can be seen in our day-to-day language. Think about when you describe an unpredictable person who has a volatile nature: most people would refer to that as a "Jekyll and Hyde" personality. The author, Robert Louis Stevenson, developed the story after years of playing with the idea of how personality can express good or evil.

One of his direct sources of inspiration may have been his friendship with a French teacher he once knew who was convicted of murdering his wife with opium. Stevenson attended the trial, amazed at how someone who was so normal in his day-to-day life could commit such an atrocity.

Murder? Madness? Mystery? Those are Wednesday's favorite subjects. This book rolls all three of those into one in a very surprising and complex way.

Pages where quotations appear: 38, 56, 98, 156

THE TRAGEDY OF MACBETH

By William Shakespeare
Originally published in 1623

Macbeth is the tragedy of a Scottish general named Macbeth whose political ambition consumes him and his family and ultimately leads to his downfall. When three witches tell Macbeth that he will one day be the king of Scotland, he returns home to tell his wife. With her desire for power adding fuel to the fire, Macbeth eventually murders the current king of Scotland and takes his place on the throne. The play explores the detrimental effects of ambition and the pursuit of power for its own sake on people, as well as those around them.

Wednesday's fascination with Macbeth may not be just because of her love of all things witchcraft; Macbeth's descent into madness and evil is a particular interest for Wednesday. The limits the human psyche can push itself to with only the slightest nudge (e.g., a couple of old witches with a cauldron) inspires her. And it could happen to anyone—a friend, a classmate, a brother.

Pages where quotations appear: 44, 50, 104, 112

THE GRIMM BROTHERS' CHILDREN'S AND HOUSEHOLD TALES

By Jacob Grimm and Wilhelm Grimm
Originally published in 1812 and 1815

The Grimm brothers were born in Germany and were touched by tragedy early on in their lives. When their father passed away suddenly, Jacob Grimm was forced to become head of the household at the age of eleven. Their family had to tighten belts; however, when Jacob and Wilhelm came of age, their aunt sent them to a very prestigious high school. While there, they set about becoming the best students in their class in order to one day support their family. Both brothers excelled and became heads of their class.

After college, the Grimm brothers became fascintated with German literature and were asked by friends to begin writing down oral stories as sort of a historical preservation project. The brothers set about this task, and thus *The Grimm Brothers' Children's and Household Tales* was born.

We all know the typical fairy tales: Cinderella marries the prince, the princess kisses the frog, and Rapunzel gets her man by using her hair. But the Grimm brothers tell these stories a bit differently. They are more tragic and have a little more gore—let's face it: lots of gore. This is why Wednesday loves to revisit these old stories: it reminds her that behind every lovely story is a much darker cautionary tale.

Pages where quotations appear: 32, 46, 60, 148

DRACULA

By Bram Stoker
Originally published in 1897

Dracula is the tale of a count who moves from Transylvania to England to feed upon the unsuspecting. He can also spread his "undead curse" to the victims, making them vampires thirsty for human blood. Cliché, right? Well, Stoker's *Dracula* was actually the first vampire novel to take all of the typical elements we know of vampires today and put them all in one book. Also, remember the "year without a summer" (a.k.a., the summer that Lord Byron, Percy Shelley, and Mary Wollstonecraft Shelley sat around telling horror stories for a competition)? Well, Lord Byron's doctor took pieces of Lord Byron's story and published them in a novel titled *The Vampyre*. This novel would later influence Stoker while he was writing *Dracula*, the most influential and successful vampire story of all time. Small world, right?

It's not surprising that Wednesday would keep a copy of *Dracula* in her library. The story of the old count is as exciting as it is informative. One must always be knowledgeable about vampires in case of chance encounters.

Pages where quotations appear: 52, 66, 90, 102

THE SCARLET LETTER

By Nathaniel Hawthorne
Originally published in 1850

The Scarlet Letter is historical fiction and set in seventeenth-century Massachusetts. The story opens on Hester Prynne, a Puritan woman who has had an affair outside of marriage and given birth to a daughter.

Her community tries to force her to name her lover and wear the red letter "A" to mark her as an adulteress. Hester's struggle for a normal life shows us the power social shaming has over an individual's life, whether they like it or not.

Wednesday has always been a fan of scaffolds. So much can happen on a scaffold. When a book opens with a woman on a scaffold like this one does, it can be an inspiring image to someone like Wednesday, who may not be as pious and forgiving as Hester.

Pages where quotations appear: 58, 78, 124, 130

THE PICTURE OF DORIAN GRAY

By Oscar Wilde
Originally published in Lippincott's
Monthly Magazine *in 1890*

The Picture of Dorian Gray is a philosophical novel that follows the larger-than-life character Dorian Gray. When Dorian has his portrait painted, the artist is entranced by his beauty in the portrait. Dorian adopts a hedonistic worldview, seeking pleasure and beauty for fulfillment, and sells his soul so that his portrait ages but he never does. This idea of indulging in life's pleasure was vulgar to the people in Victorian England, and the story was quickly censored by the literary magazine.

Not only was his novel considered profane, but Oscar Wilde's life was also considered unfit for normal English society. His choice to live as a gay man wasn't taken lightly, as homosexuality at the time was a criminal offense. Only five years after publishing *The Picture of Dorian Gray*, Oscar Wilde was imprisoned for this "offense."

Pages where quotations appear: 26, 74, 86, 116

WUTHERING HEIGHTS

By Emily Brontë
Originally published in 1847

Wuthering Heights was Emily Brontë's only novel. She published it in 1847, under a different name. She used the pseudonym "Ellis Bell." Emily Brontë came from a talented family. Her sister Anne published a novel called *Agnes Grey*, and their sister Charlotte published *Jane Eyre*, which is also quoted in this book.

Wuthering Heights is the story of a doomed love affair between two pretty unpleasant people. People love it now, but at the time of its publication, some people really hated it. By the standards of the time, the book is dark, intense, and overwhelmingly passionate. The English poet and painter Dante Gabriel Rossetti said it was "a fiend of a book—an incredible monster."

It may not surprise you to learn that Wednesday, a passionate young woman, is a huge fan of this book about passionate young people. Plus, anything that can be described as "a fiend of a book" is obviously right up her alley.

Pages where quotations appear: 80, 92, 118, 134

THE DIVINE COMEDY

By Dante Alighieri
Published as Divina Commedia *in 1555*

The Divine Comedy is a very long Italian poem by Dante Alighieri, who died one year after finishing work on it. It is probably the most famous work of Italian literature and is thought to be one of the greatest works of world literature. The poem describes Dante's imagined travels through hell, purgatory, and paradise. He is guided on this journey by the ancient poet Virgil.

Wednesday is especially fond of the poem's very, very detailed descriptions of hell. Wednesday loves anything ugly, scary, or twisted, and Dante's hell is all of those things.

Pages where quotations appear: 82, 84, 94, 154

"THE LEGEND OF SLEEPY HOLLOW"

By Washington Irving
Originally published in 1820

Set in a famously haunted and spooky part of New York State, "The Legend of Sleepy Hollow" tells the story of a nervous schoolteacher named Ichabod Crane, who has a mysterious run-in with a headless horseman. Ichabod disappears forever after crossing paths with the horseman ... did he just come to his senses and find a new place to live? Or did the horseman spirit him away to some other realm?

Wednesday might know, but she isn't telling. Anyway, she lives in New Jersey, not New York.

Pages where quotations appear: 106, 114, 152, 162

JANE EYRE

By Charlotte Brontë
Originally published in 1847

Another Brontë sister rears her head. This one is Charlotte, and she's best remembered for *Jane Eyre*, a gothic novel about a governess who goes to work in a spooky house where something is very, very wrong. This book blew people's minds when it was published because it gave them such a powerful view into the inner life of its passionate young protagonist.

Jane has a strong interest in the supernatural, which is probably one of the reasons Wednesday likes this book so much. There's also the fact that Jane is an odd-looking person who seems to resemble a fairy or a sprite, just like—you guessed it—Wednesday!

Pages where quotations appear: 34, 70, 132, 174

LES MISÉRABLES

By Victor Hugo
Originally published in 1862

Many people think *Les Misérables* is one of the greatest novels of the nineteenth century. It follows the lives of a large cast of characters over a period of seventeen years. Contrary to popular belief, the book ends not with the French Revolution but the June Rebellion of 1832, an anti-monarchist uprising. The focus of the book is the life and difficulties of Jean Valjean, an ex-convict looking for redemption.

The novel is about lots of different things: law, the history of France, politics, religion, love ... But the reason Wednesday loves it so much is that it's also about suffering. So very, very, very much suffering.

Pages where quotations appear: 120, 128, 158, 176

POEMS
By Emily Dickinson

"Because I could not stop for Death –"
Originally published in 1890
"Safe in their Alabaster Chambers –"
Originally published in 1890
"I heard a Fly buzz – when I died –"
Originally published in 1896
"I felt a Funeral, in my Brain,"
Originally published in 1896

One of the great American poets of the nineteenth century, Emily Dickinson wrote nearly 1,800 poems. Fewer than a dozen of these poems were published during her life—her fame really occurred after she had died. She became very reclusive toward the end of her life, often refusing to meet people face-to-face and speaking to them through closed doors instead. She would frequently dress in all white, and her neighbors found her to be a thoroughly spooky presence in the area.

Wednesday loves Emily Dickinson for all of these reasons, but the thing she loves the most is the fact that Dickinson was obsessed with death—particularly her own—and wrote a great number of poems on the subject.

Pages where quotations appear: 126, 136, 140, 146

THE CASTLE OF OTRANTO

By Horace Walpole
Originally published in 1764

The Castle of Otranto is the very first gothic novel ever written. In the second edition of the book, Walpole changed the subtitle to "A Gothic Story." The novel combined horror and a medieval style in a way that gothic novels have been doing ever since.

Otranto created a genre that became very popular in the nineteenth century. Authors like Mary Wollstonecraft Shelley, Bram Stoker, Edgar Allan Poe, and Charlotte Brontë all worked in the gothic genre. (Do those names ring a bell, dear reader?)

Wednesday included *The Castle of Otranto* in this book because she knows how important it is to respect the classics. When you're a goth, you're a goth all the way ... and that means knowing your roots.

Pages where quotations appear: 144, 150, 166, 172

HAMLET, PRINCE OF DENMARK

By William Shakespeare
Originally published in 1603

The Tragedy of Hamlet, Prince of Denmark is the full title, but it's often just referred to as *Hamlet*. A tragedy set in Denmark, the play tells the story of how Prince Hamlet seeks revenge on his uncle, Claudius, at the bidding of the ghost of his murdered father.

Hamlet is the longest play Shakespeare ever wrote, and is one of the most famous works of literature in the world. It's a retelling of the legend of Amleth, a character in a medieval Scandinavian legend.

One of the most famous scenes in *Hamlet* is set in a graveyard, where Hamlet talks to a human skull and considers suicide. Three guesses what Wednesday's favorite scene is . . .

Pages where quotations appear: 30, 76, 138, 180

PARADISE LOST

By John Milton
Originally published in 1667

Paradise Lost is an epic poem written in blank verse that retells the biblical stories of the fall of Adam and Eve and the fall of Satan. At the ripe old age of sixty, the English poet John Milton published the work in ten books. In this epic (and I mean EPIC) retelling of these old Bible stories, Milton wants to dramatize and humanize the characters of God, Satan, Adam, and Eve for readers. He takes these stories that everyone knows and puts them in a storytelling structure reminiscent of classic battles between kings, making his work relatable to his readership at the time.

The poem is essential to Wednesday's library, as it provides her with a story where Satan is the hero, something that no one had ever really done before. The evolution of evil is important to learn about, especially when one is looking to follow a similar path.

Pages where quotations appear: 42, 64, 160, 164

THE WORKS OF EDGAR ALLAN POE

By Edgar Allan Poe

"The Raven"
Originally published in 1845 in the New York Evening Mirror
"The Tell-Tale Heart"
Originally published in 1843 in The Pioneer
"Berenice"
Originally published in 1835 in Southern Literary Messenger
"The Pit and Pendulum"
Originally published in 1842 in The Gift: A Christmas and New Year's Present for 1843
"A Dream Within a Dream"
Originally published in 1849 in The Flag of Our Union
"Annabel Lee"
Originally published in 1849 in New York Tribune
"The Fall of the House of Usher"
Originally published in 1839 in Burton's Gentleman's Magazine

Edgar Allan Poe is best known for his macabre poetry and short stories that were published in periodicals and literary journals between 1835 and his sudden death in 1849. He was one of the first well-known American writers and earned a living solely from his writing career. This made his life very difficult to navigate financially. Not only did he have money problems, but a decade after he married his thirteen-year-old cousin Virginia Clemm, she tragically died from tuberculosis.

Virginia's death had a profound effect on Poe. This is what is believed to have inspired "Annabel Lee," a poem about a man whose love dies from a cold. His wife's death may have also inspired "A Dream Within a Dream," where the speaker laments the fact that the important things in life seem to slip away so quickly. However, Poe had always had this bleak outlook on life: starting with "Berenice" in 1835, and continuing through "The Fall of the House of Usher," then "The Pit and the Pendulum," and finally the "The Tell-Tale Heart." It's clear that Poe had an obsession with the power of the human mind, specifically, the power the human mind had when it was pushed to its limits and driven to madness. Poe didn't reach critical acclaim until he published "The Raven," taking this idea of madness and putting it in such a masterfully simple scenario of a man driven to insanity by a raven.

As someone who enjoys living in a haunted former insane asylum, Wednesday has a great deal of appreciation for stories about madness, dead people's teeth, and creepy houses where scary, inexplicable disasters occur. And Poe is one of her favorite writers—as you might have noticed from leafing through this book!

Pages where quotations appear: 15–24, 48, 72, 88, 96, 100, 110, 122, 168, 182–184